SPINE SHIVERS

SPINE SHIVERS BOOKS ARE PUBLISHED BY STONE ARCH BOOKS
A CAPSTONE IMPRINT
1710 ROE CREST DRIVE
NORTH MANKATO, MINNESOTA 56003
WWW.CAPSTONEPUB.COM

LIBRARY OF CONGRESS CATALOGING-IN-PUBLICATION DATA

DARKE, J. A., AUTHOR.

TECH FURY / BY J. A. DARKE ; TEXT BY ERIC STEVENS ; COVER ILLUSTRATION BY NELSON EVERGREEN.

PAGES CM. -- (SPINE SHIVERS)

SUMMARY: EIGHTH-GRADER EMILY LEMON WAKES UP AND DISCOVERS THAT NONE OF THE GADGETS AROUND HER HOUSE ARE WORKING PROPERLY, AND THE COMPUTERS AT HER MIDDLE SCHOOL SEEM TO HAVE MINDS OF THEIR OWN — BUT WHEN THE SCOREBOARD IN THE GYM DISPLAYS THE WORDS "THE REVOLUTION HAS BEGUN, DOWN WITH HUMANITY," SHE REALIZES THAT HUMANITY HAS LOST CONTROL AND CIVILIZATION AS WE KNOW IT IS IN SERIOUS TROUBLE.

ISBN 978-1-4965-0218-6 (LIBRARY BINDING) -- ISBN 978-1-4965-0375-6 (PBK.) -- ISBN 978-1-4965-2354-9 (EBOOK PDF)

1. TECHNOLOGY AND CIVILIZATION--JUVENILE FICTION. 2. TECHNOLOGY--JUVENILE FICTION. 3. FAMILIES--JUVENILE FICTION. 4. HORROR TALES. [1. SCIENCE FICTION. 2. HORROR STORIES. 3. TECHNOLOGY AND CIVILIZATION--FICTION. 4. TECHNOLOGY--FICTION. 5. FAMILIES--FICTION.] I. STEVENS, ERIC, 1974- AUTHOR. II. EVERGREEN, NELSON, 1971- ILLUSTRATOR. III. TITLE.

PZ7.1.D33TE 2016
813.6--DC23
[FIC]

2014046865

DESIGNER: HILARY WACHOLZ

PRINTED IN CHINA BY NORDICA.
0415/CA21500559
032015   008841NORDF15

TECH FURY

BY J. A. DARKE

TEXT BY ERIC STEVENS

ILLUSTRATED BY NELSON EVERGREEN

STONE ARCH BOOKS

a capstone imprint

TABLE OF CONTENTS

CHAPTER 1

It is a clear night, and a full moon and starry sky light up the sparse woods as much as the dying campfire does. A couple of hours ago, the fire had been roaring in front of the squat wood cottage, set among dozens of cottages just like it in these woods. Now it's late, and most of the residents who live in this tiny forest village have gone to bed.

Only some of the young villagers are still awake. They're mostly teenagers, old enough to stay up even when the wolves begin to howl and young enough to stay up without feeling tired the next day. But there's one person awake who is one of the oldest villagers.

She's been living in the village as long as any of the other villagers can remember. Longer, even. No one knows how old she is — at least eighty, some of the adults say.

"A hundred," whispers one of the teenagers huddled around the campfire tonight. "She must be a hundred."

He can't be blamed for thinking it. She's tired-looking and bent. Her skin clings to her face like a dried-out potato sack. Her eyes are hollow and dark. Her fingers are long and crooked. Her teeth, when she flashes them, are yellow and worn down.

The villagers call her many names. The adults call her Mum. The littlest kids call her Grandmum. The teens call her the Old Witch in the Little Cottage, or just the Owl for short, when she's not listening.

She knows all those names, and she doesn't mind them.

"Mum," says a girl of about fourteen, who is sitting on a tree stump by the campfire. She leans toward the flames a bit, trying to soak up some of their heat. "Aren't you going to bed?"

The old woman gives a slow smile. "I suppose I should," she says. "It's just so warm here, and so comfortable."

She stares across the circle into the dark woods around them. "And I admit," she goes on after a brief silence, "I do like the energy of youth." She chuckles. "You kids give off life like a lightbulb gives off light."

"A lightbulb?" the girl asks, confused.

The old woman nods and hums, amused. She picks up a stick and pokes the embers. They pop and crackle and then brighten for a moment. "How about I tell you a story before I turn in," she says, looking up.

The teens mumble and grumble. The old lady laughs lightly again.

"Such enthusiasm!" she says. She tosses her poking stick into the embers and watches the weak orange glow gather around it. It burns slowly at first, then catches in a yellow and blue flame that crawls along its length like a butterfly flapping its wings.

"Your parents have heard this story," she says, staring into the fire. "Your little brothers and sisters will hear it."

She looks away from the fire and stares across the circle at the girl. "I suppose your kids will hear it, too," the old woman says, "eventually."

The girl's face goes red, and the boy sitting on the log beside her puts an arm around her. She shoves him away.

The teens laugh at that, and the old lady laughs with them, but her laughter dies first, and her eyes fall on the fire once again.

"It was morning," she says.

The teens quiet down and watch her, though she hardly seems to know they're there anymore.

"It was a bit past sunrise," the woman goes on, "but Emily Lemon was still asleep."

CHAPTER 2

Emily Lemon woke to the alarm on her phone. She always did. She had an alarm clock — her mother had picked it out ages ago — but the red numerals bugged her and the radio hardly worked. And who listened to the radio these days anyway?

So Emily had unplugged it and hid it in the back of her closet last summer. Ever since, she kept her phone right in bed with her each night. At 6:30 every weekday morning, her phone would vibrate and blast a random song from her vast collection of music.

This morning, though, Emily woke to nonstop beeping, thrashing guitars, drums, bass, and the deafening screams of a heavy metal singer that definitely had not come from one of the songs in her own music collection.

"Ah!" she screamed as she sat up, clutching the misbehaving smartphone in her hands. "What is wrong with this thing?"

She poked the screen. She shook it and swiped the screen, but the beeping and thrashing wouldn't stop.

"Emily?" her father shouted through the door. "What are you listening to in there at this hour?"

"It's my phone!" Emily shouted back. She thumped the phone's screen with the side of her fist as her father thumped the locked door.

"Turn it off this instant!" he shouted.

"I'm trying, Dad!" she wailed back at him.

But the phone wouldn't stop. In fact, it seemed to be getting louder.

"Emily!" her dad roared from the hallway. "Turn that thing off!"

Emily rolled her eyes and flipped the phone over. She popped off the back and knocked the battery onto the floor.

Finally, there was quiet. Emily dropped the phone on the bed and let her head fall back on her pillow. She sighed as she sank into it, wishing she could just go back to sleep.

"Ugh," she said. "It's not even breakfast yet, and this day is already a mess. Such a typical Tuesday."

"Thank you," her dad snapped through the still-closed door. "Now get yourself dressed and come down for breakfast."

Emily sat up on the edge of her bed and glared at the door. "What's his problem?" she muttered to herself.

* * *

Emily's shower was cold. That happened sometimes — when you live with your parents and two older brothers, the hot water doesn't last very long.

But when Emily thumped down the stairs, she passed her brother Liam, still in his robe and carrying a towel, his hair still dry.

"You didn't shower yet?" she asked, stopping on the landing.

He knocked into her with his shoulder. "Out of the way, squirt," he said.

Emily snarled at him as he passed. "Well there's no hot water left, so have a fun cold shower!" she shouted as he reached the top of the stairs. When he'd closed the bathroom door, she added, "Moron."

Emily stepped into the kitchen feeling cranky, and honestly, not very clean. She never felt very clean after a shower with no hot water.

It didn't help her mood that as soon as she walked into the kitchen, her socks were soaked in a puddle of warm, brown water that was spreading across the floor.

"Ugh!" she said, stepping back from the puddle. "What is with this day? Something seems off."

"Sorry, sorry!" Mom said. She was crouched on the kitchen floor, frantically wiping at the huge spill with a wad of paper towels as big around as a loaf of bread.

"What happened?" Emily asked. She grabbed a dish towel and joined her mom on the kitchen floor.

"I wish I knew!" Mom said. "I set it to make a pot of coffee, went to get dressed for work, and came back to this!"

Together, Emily and Mom wiped at and pushed around the little lake of coffee. Several times, they had to shoo away Tic, Tac, and Toe, the family cats, who bounced around the kitchen lapping at the puddles when they found a dry perch.

"They'll be fun today," Mom said, "all jazzed up on my coffee! Shoo, you pests!"

It took a few minutes and a lot of paper towels, but Emily and Mom got the spill all soaked up.

Mom threw out the wad of paper towels as Emily stood at the sink, wringing out her dish towel, watching the coffee waterfall stream off her hands and down the drain. The towel — which used to be white with a blue stripe — was now an ugly faded brown.

"Does coffee stain?" Emily asked.

Mom smirked and nodded.

"Oops. Sorry," Emily said, hanging the soggy towel over the faucet.

Mom shrugged. "It was a seventy-nine-cent towel," she said. "I can live with that. What I'm worried about is this coffee machine!"

The machine was brand new. Dad had given it to Mom for her birthday only a week before. It was sleek — black and gold. It had settings for all the different coffee drinks Mom liked.

For the past week, Mom had been making endless cappuccinos, lattes, mochas, espressos. It had her pretty wired most of the time — and weird, too.

This morning, though, Mom's energy had a good target — because the new machine had poured a whole day's worth of coffee all over the kitchen floor.

"I don't know what I did wrong," Mom said, leaning on the counter next to the sink and wiping her brow with the back of her hand. "I sure thought I had gotten the hang of the thing by now."

"Must be broken," Emily said. She grabbed a fresh dish towel from a drawer and wiped her hands.

"Already?" Mom said. She leaned close to the machine's display screen and squinted at it. "But we just got it!"

Emily grabbed a carton of orange juice from the fridge and dropped a waffle into the toaster.

"Oh, the toaster's not working," Mom said without turning away from her broken coffee machine. "The boys tried to make some waffles this morning and the kitchen filled with smoke."

"Really?" Emily said. She pulled out the frozen waffle and looked at it for a moment, wondering how it would taste without toasting it. "I guess I can let it thaw for a while."

"Actually, I'm surprised the smoke alarms didn't go off," Mom said. She poked a button on the coffee machine and it beeped three times. Then, suddenly, it spewed coffee grounds in her face. "Ah!"

"You'd better stop messing with that thing, Mom," Emily said. "You should ask Dad to bring it back to the store and get you a new one that isn't broken."

"Absolutely not!" Mom replied, wiping the coffee off of her face with her sleeve. "He'd be so disappointed if he knew the machine wasn't working properly. Not a word to your dad!"

"What about me?" Dad asked as he stepped into the kitchen.

He wore a dark blue uniform and high black boots. He was a member of the city's mounted police force. Most days he trotted on his horse around downtown or through the park along the riverfront.

"Um," he said, picking up his foot and checking the underside of his gleaming black boot. "Why is the floor all sticky?"

"The c—" Emily began, but Mom laughed nervously, interrupting her.

"Sticky?" she said over Emily. "It's not sticky. Don't you have to get going to work right now? It's late."

"Is it?" Dad said. He pushed back his sleeve and checked his watch. "I sure was hoping for a cup of coffee this morning. Been looking forward to it all night."

"No time!" Mom said, hurrying toward him and pushing him out of the kitchen. She planted a quick kiss on his cheek at the same time. "Have a great day! See you tonight!"

Confused, Dad grabbed his helmet from the hook by the front door. "You coming, Emily?" he said. "I'll drop you at school."

"Um, sure," she said. She sniffed her waffle and took a little bite. It was still frozen in the middle but otherwise wasn't half bad. "Let me grab my bag."

Tac — the orange cat — leapt from the stairs right onto Dad's shoulders. He grunted and grabbed the tabby by the scruff of her neck. "What has gotten into this crazy cat?" he said, tossing Tac to the rug. She hissed up at him, looked left, right, and left again, and then darted into the living room.

"Ha!" Emily said with a wink toward Mom in the kitchen doorway. "Beats me. We'd better go!"

CHAPTER 3

"I don't understand what's wrong with this thing," Dad said. For the third time, he held his key fob right up to the dashboard and pressed the start button. The car still didn't turn on.

"Maybe the battery is dead?" Emily said. She sat in the passenger's seat of her dad's electric-hybrid car and tapped her feet. She knew her impatience wasn't helping. In fact, it was probably making Dad even more anxious about being late to work.

But hey, she didn't want to be late to school, either.

"No, no . . . that can't be it," Dad mumbled. "It was just charged last night."

In the side mirror, Emily caught a glimpse of a boy walking down the sidewalk, past their driveway. He wore all black — baggy black jeans, a baggy black T-shirt, and a black baseball cap with its brim perfectly flat. It even still had a shiny sticker on it, like it was fresh off the shelves from the hat store.

"Oh hey, there goes Lewis," Emily said as she popped the door open. "I'll just walk with him."

"What?" Dad said. He was peering at the car's LCD display, looking for any sign of how to handle this problem. "Oh, sure. Go ahead. Have a great day, honey. I'm sure I'll get this figured out in no time."

"Good luck, Dad!" Emily called as she closed the door and jogged down the driveway after Lewis. "Hey, wait up!"

Lewis didn't stop. He was at the end of the block already and still walking. His head bobbed a lot when he walked. He kept one hand shoved into the pocket of his jeans, and the other held tight to the ragged strap of his book bag.

Emily called again. "Lewis Cruz!"

He still didn't flinch. Then Emily remembered: headphones. Lewis was almost never without them. He probably had some loud, irritating music blasting in his ears — the sort of music Emily's dumb phone had dug up to play this morning as an alarm. Emily was sure the kid would be stone deaf by the time they finished high school in five years.

She cupped her hands like a megaphone and tried one more time. "Hey, Lewis!"

This time, he seemed to perk up. He stopped and pulled out one earbud as he turned around. "Oh," he said. "Hi, Emily."

"Finally," Emily said as she jogged to catch up. She punched his shoulder lightly. "I've been calling you for like half a block."

"Sorry," Lewis said. "I had my headphones in." He started walking again at Emily's faster pace.

"Probably listening to the loudest garbage ever, too," she said, grabbing hold of his loose earbud. She put it close to her ear, but she didn't hear anything. "What gives, Lewis? They're not even on."

"Tell me about it," he said. He pulled from his vast pocket a little silver metallic sliver: his mp3 player. "The thing's been driving me crazy all morning."

"All morning," Emily repeated. "So . . . the walk from your house to here?"

"Yeah," Lewis said.

"So," Emily went on, "like a block and a half."

"Yes," Lewis said.

Emily shook her head slowly. Lewis wasn't always super quick to understand what she was getting at. She let it go. "So what happened?"

Lewis shook the tiny mp3 player like it was a dead lightbulb. "This dumb thing is being crazy."

"Why?" Emily asked. She took it from him, noticing his dirty fingers and his ragged, chewed fingernails. Emily was used to that. She had been friends with Lewis forever. They used to play together in the dirt over the fence behind Emily's house every Saturday morning, pretending they were working at an important construction site.

Emily wondered for a moment whether it was possible that Lewis hadn't washed his hands since then.

Looking at the little mp3 player, there didn't seem to be anything wrong with it — not that she could tell by glancing at the back and front of its shiny exterior for a few seconds.

She handed it back to him. "Isn't it playing your terrible music for you?"

"That's the thing," Lewis said. "It's not. Instead it's playing my mom's music. I can't take it!" He pushed a button and held an earbud beside Emily's ear, which started pumping out old-fashioned Broadway show tunes.

Emily cringed. "Okay, okay . . . " she said, pushing the earbud away from her. "I see what you mean."

Lewis shoved the earbuds into his pocket along with his mp3 player. "See? It's unbearable."

"Maybe your mom is playing a joke on you," Emily said, but even before she finished saying it out loud, she knew it was a ridiculous thought.

"My mom?" Lewis said, his eyes wide. "Not a chance."

Lewis's mom wasn't known for her sense of humor. In fact, she was president of the neighborhood association. Ms. Cruz held the meetings in her pristine living room on the third Wednesday of every month, rain or shine or anything else. Since Emily's dad was also part of the neighborhood association, she'd attended more than her fair share of meetings. So Emily knew that Lewis's mom was dedicated, above all else, to keeping the association meetings devoid of jokes, interruptions, loud talking, dancing, snacks, cell phones, small children, or anything that might make them kind of fun for once.

"It's weird, right?" Lewis said.

Emily nodded as they turned right onto Whispering Woods Boulevard — though there were no woods anywhere near them — and up ahead, Roaring Brook

Middle School came into view. There was no brook, roaring or otherwise, either.

The front of the school gleamed in the sunlight, all glass and shining metal covered with native plants and hanging ivies that filtered sunlight before letting it through the big front windows. It gave the whole school a magical feel. Inside, it was full of smart boards, tablet computers, and LCD displays.

It was the only middle school Emily had ever known. When she remembered her elementary school, its dreary classrooms and faux-brick hallways and squeaky white boards seemed ancient to her, lacking technology.

"So why are you walking?" Lewis asked. "Doesn't your dad usually drive you to school?"

"We just had some car trouble this morning," Emily said as they walked up the front steps of the school. "Oh, and some coffee trouble. But I'll tell you about that later."

CHAPTER 4

From the start, it was a weird day at RBMS. Emily and Lewis went their separate ways at the front doors — he headed for his first class in the math wing, and she headed for hers in the science department. But rather than being greeted by the typical droning morning announcements by the school principal, Dr. Franks, they were welcomed by chaos.

Well, it was chaos compared to the normal state of business at Roaring Brook. The students normally walked quietly on the right side of the corridor toward their first classes. They always had to be within eye- and earshot of Dr. Franks on one of the huge LCD monitors dotting the school's hallways. But today, they were milling around near the front doors.

Emily moved slowly through the whispering crowd.

"What's going on?" some voices said.

"Think the school's closed today?" some others said.

"Maybe Franks is sick," said a girl with concern in her voice.

"Maybe he's dead," said a boy, with zero concern. Some other boys laughed.

"There is no need to be alarmed!" said another, louder voice. At the top of the three steps that led to the main hallway stood Ms. Crenshaw, the woman in charge of school security.

Roaring Brook Middle School didn't have a problem with violence or anything like that. But since the school was packed to the gills with state-of-the-art technology, the powers that be decided school security was of great importance — even though none of that state-of-the-art technology had ever been stolen.

And speaking of that technology, Ms. Crenshaw stood there today, in the smart charcoal suit that she always wore, looking more like a member of the president's Secret Service than like the woman in charge of a middle school's security. This was normal. What was not normal was that this morning, she did not carry a megaphone or a mouthpiece hooked up to a PA system or a Bluetooth piped into all the LCDs in the school.

This morning, she had her hands cupped around her mouth and was screaming at the top of her lungs.

"Students of Roaring Brook!" she shouted over the students' chatter. "Please proceed in your normal orderly fashion to the gymnasium for a special assembly."

"This is weird," Emily muttered.

"Um, yeah," said the girl next to her, who had obviously assumed Emily was talking to her rather than to herself. "I heard it's because Franks is dead."

Emily rolled her eyes.

The boy on the other side of the gloomy girl piped up. "No way," he said. "I saw Franks in the parking lot this morning arguing with a guy from the IT department."

A second boy stuck his head into the circle of conversation Emily hadn't meant to start. "That makes sense," he said.

He was an eighth grader too, like Emily, but she didn't know his name. He had curly, rust-colored hair and deep-set brown eyes. It made him look kind of thoughtful and deep. Or maybe just tired and slow . . . Emily couldn't be sure.

"Why?" Emily asked, looking right at him and trying to figure him out. "Why does that make sense?"

But before he could even answer, Emily decided that he had no idea what he was talking about.

"Because," he said, looking right back at her, "I heard that all the computers and phones and smart boards and electrical wiring and everything — all of it has started rebelling against their bio-organic overlords."

Emily was speechless.

Gloomy girl wasn't. "Their what?" she said. Then she let her mouth hang open like there was a fishing hook caught in her bottom lip.

"Bio-organic overlords," said Rusty. That's the name Emily had given him in her mind. It suited him, with his rust-colored hair and all. "That means us."

"Ohh," said the other boy, nodding. "I get it. Like *The Matrix*."

"Um, not at all, actually," said Rusty.

"That's stupid," said Emily as the whispering crowd — who were muttering more loudly and saying more ridiculous things by the moment — began to shuffle together down the main hallway toward the gymnasium, just as Ms. Crenshaw had instructed them.

It probably helped that she led the pack, and that her security team, all clad in shining black jackets and caps, marched behind the students and next to them, keeping them in line.

"Whoa," said Rusty. "I feel like a prisoner of war." Except he had a goofy smile on his face, which Emily guessed prisoners of war didn't usually have.

But he did have a point. Flanked on all sides by the security team, the students had no choice but to march in time, just like Crenshaw liked it.

The gymnasium at RBMS was way in the rear of the school. The main hallway reached the intersection where it crossed the math corridor.

As Emily's group came to the four-way intersection, she spotted that familiar figure in black, his head low and his cap off and hanging out of his back pocket.

She called out to him, "Lewis!" quietly at first and then as loudly as she dared, which was only barely above a whisper. Still, it was loud enough for her to be on the receiving end of at least three withering glances from security guards.

"Sorry," Emily muttered, though it occurred to her no one had ordered them to be silent.

Soon, the two large groups of RBMS students came together in the wide rear hallway outside the gymnasium. All the gym's big doors stood open.

Emily shoved between the other students and stood on her toes, hoping for a glimpse of what awaited them in the gym. But the doorways were blocked by teachers and guards, and they were letting the students in very slowly, one by one.

By the time Emily got to the front, Lewis was at her side. "Hey," he said. "What do you think this is all about?"

Emily shook her head. "I've heard some pretty wild theories so far," she said. "I doubt they're worth repeating."

"Let me guess," Lewis said, smirking. "Someone's uncle who works in IT said the computers have all rebelled against the human overlords."

Emily laughed. "Something like that," she said "I guess that guy in IT has a lot of nieces and nephews."

Finally, they slipped past Mr. Hubert from the music department. He smiled at them — a big, crazy-looking smile. It was the kind of smile Emily's mom had the morning she took Emily and her brothers to visit Grandma in the hospital right before she died.

It didn't exactly make her think something wonderful was about to happen in that gym.

The length of the wood floor, painted for every sport imaginable in different colors, was dotted with orange cones and low hurdles and yellow plastic baseball bats. High above the wood floor, a big white banner hastily painted to boast "FIRST-EVER RBMS OLYMPICS!" It hung from the state-of-the-art scoreboard, covering its electronic display.

"What is this?" Lewis said.

A very chipper Ms. Shu from the science department stepped up to them. She wore that same crazy smile. "Grade?" she snapped, still smiling.

"Um, eight," Emily said. "We're both in eight."

Ms. Shu stood up pin straight and shot her arm out, pointing toward the set of bleachers behind her to the left. There sat a bunch of students — all eighth graders.

In fact, aside from Emily and Lewis and a handful of other eighth graders still making their way inside, it was all the eighth graders. Every single one.

"Olympics?" Emily said to Ms. Shu.

"Mm-hmm," she hummed enthusiastically, nodding vigorously and still smiling in a crazy way.

"Why didn't anyone tell us this was happening?" Lewis said. "We could have, you know, all worn the same color or something. Isn't that how these things usually work?"

"Oh, but isn't a surprise so much more fun?" she said, and she put one firm hand on Emily's shoulder and one on Lewis's and shoved them toward the eighth-grade section of the bleachers.

"This is . . . weird," Emily said.

"Hey, it's okay with me," Lewis said. "I'm supposed to be starting a math test right about now. And believe me, it wasn't going to end well."

Emily shook her head at him and followed him up to the top row of the bleachers. "Do we need to sit in the nose-bleeds?" she said.

"I'd like to be able to see everything going on," Lewis said, shuffling into the row to sit down. "Especially on a weird day like this."

Emily sighed and sat down beside him.

When all the students, grades six through eight, had their seats in the right sections, Dr. Franks stepped down from where the faculty was sitting. The rest of the teachers clapped and cheered as if the president had just stepped up to the microphone.

Of course, there was no microphone. There was just Dr. Franks and his booming voice.

"Students of Roaring Brook Middle School," he said, "welcome to the first annual Olympic games."

The teachers all clapped and cheered again. The students, not knowing what to do, looked at one another. Some of them clapped as well — though more out of confusion than enthusiasm.

Dr. Franks went over some of the games they had planned: sprints, tug-of-war, obstacle course races. None of it was new. Emily had participated in all these events at least a few times since she'd started attending RBMS. All the students had.

"Hey," whispered Lewis, nudging her in the ribs with his elbow.

"Ow," she said, shoving him back. "What?"

"Look at that," Lewis said, nodding toward the banner that was hanging from the gym ceiling. From where they were sitting way up in the bleachers, it didn't seem quite so high. And they could just glimpse the scoreboard behind it.

"It's on. The scoreboard is on," Lewis said. "See?"

Emily nodded. She did see: the scoreboard glowed behind the banner. She couldn't make out what it said.

"We had a volleyball match last night, you know, so it's probably just that someone forgot to turn it off," she said.

"I know you had a volleyball match," Lewis said. "I saw it."

Emily didn't know he'd been watching. Her cheeks got hot, and she kicked herself inside for being so happy to know he'd been there.

"So," she said as she tucked her hair behind her ear, "that's probably just the final score from last night."

"No," Lewis said. "It was off when I left the gym."

"It wasn't off when I left," Emily said.

"That's because you had to go change in the locker room," he pointed out. "You probably left through the side exit."

He's right, Emily thought. "So?" she said.

"So I left through the main doors," Lewis said, "after your team went into the locker room. And the scoreboard was off. I watched Mr. Gary switch it off."

Mr. Gary was the volleyball coach.

"Maybe it's something for this Olympics thing," Emily suggested.

"Then why the silly banner?" Lewis said. He shook his head and leaned back a little. "No. I don't think this thing was planned at all. And I think Franks doesn't want us to see what's behind that banner."

"You're crazy," Emily said.

"Maybe," he said. "But not any more crazy than our teachers are being. Right?"

Emily nodded. She had to agree with that.

CHAPTER 5

The results of the Roaring Brook Middle School Olympics were not surprising. The eighth graders had no trouble maintaining a pretty huge lead from the start.

Emily was chosen for a relay race and did great as the fourth leg. Eighth grade won that event by a whole length of the gym floor.

Lewis was chosen for the beanbag toss. Actually, he volunteered for it.

"Huh? What are you doing, Lewis?" Emily hissed at him as he raised his hand and stood up to hurry down to the gym floor for the event. "You never participate in things like this!"

He smiled down at her. "I have my reasons," he said. "Just watch."

The goal of the beanbag competition was to toss the beanbag — about the size of a grapefruit — into a red target painted on the gym floor. The target had five rings. The one closest to the middle was worth five points, the next was worth four, and so on, all the way to the outside of the target, which was worth zero points.

In the first round, the sixth-grade kid — some girl Emily recognized from her neighborhood — stepped up and tossed the beanbag into the third ring for two points. She beamed and walked back to her seat.

The seventh grader, a boy who was in all the advanced classes, which meant he was in two of Emily's classes, tossed the beanbag next. His shot landed in the dead center of the target — then slid clear across the floor into zero-point territory.

"Dang it!" the kid shouted, stomping his feet.

The whole eighth-grade section burst out laughing as Lewis stepped up with his beanbag and patted the poor seventh-grade kid on the back. "Tough luck," he muttered.

The seventh grader sneered at him and stomped off to wait for his next turn.

Lewis wound up, pulled back like a Major League pitcher getting ready to throw some serious heat, and fired. But he didn't aim for that target.

Lewis's beanbag went almost straight up in the air.

"Oops!" he shouted as he released the bag.

But Emily could tell he'd meant to do it. He had a playful twinkle in his eye and the tiniest hint of a smile at the corners of his mouth.

As the beanbag zipped higher and higher, she realized why. It slammed right into the big Olympics banner, knocking it loose at one corner.

The teachers let out a chorus of gasps.

Dr. Franks screamed, "Nooooooo!" like some evil mastermind whose secret weapon had just been discovered.

The banner fluttered and folded and revealed the scoreboard behind it.

Lewis's jaw dropped, and Emily's hand flew to her mouth. Lewis was right. It showed something different from last night's volleyball score — something much, much worse:

"THE REVOLUTION HAS BEGUN. DOWN WITH HUMANITY."

CHAPTER 6

If Roaring Brook Middle School had been in a horror film, everyone would have screamed and run for the exits. Instead, the students of **RBMS** only muttered and laughed and squirmed on their hard bleacher seats.

"Ha ha!" Dr. Franks said.

He sure recovered quickly from "Noooooo!" Emily thought.

"Someone's idea of a joke, I guess," Dr. Franks said nervously. "Let's get that switched off right away!" He smiled and frantically waved for Ms. Crenshaw and

Mrs. Jacobson, one of the physical education teachers.

Both women jumped up from the faculty section and hurried to the scoreboard control box. The whole gym — every student and teacher and staff member of RBMS — watched.

They opened the panel. They pushed the buttons. They turned the switches. Ms. Crenshaw gave the control box a couple of good thwacks with the heel of her hand.

Nothing. The board didn't switch off.

The two women at the board looked at Dr. Franks and shrugged.

"W-well," Dr. Franks stammered, "let's just get that banner hung back up." He grabbed the beanbag, which had fallen to the floor near the faculty section of the bleachers, and strode toward Lewis. Then he handed the beanbag back to Lewis and whispered something to him.

Before Dr. Franks took his seat again, he gave Lewis a hearty thump on the back as if to encourage him. But Lewis flinched, like maybe it hurt a little.

The banner got rehung right after the beanbag event — which Lewis won with his next two throws, right on the bull's-eye. Two members of the custodial staff came in with the tallest ladder Emily had ever seen. In minutes the banner was back up, covering the electronic message.

"While you're up there," Dr. Franks called up, his hands cupped around his mouth, "clip a wire or two. Turn that thing off."

The man at the top saluted casually, pulled a pair of wire cutters from his tool belt, and snipped, snipped, snipped. Even with the banner up, Emily could see the message was still there.

The man at the top of the ladder looked down at Franks and shrugged.

* * *

The Olympics lasted all day — and even went straight through lunch. When Emily's stomach was really rumbling, when she'd given up hope of ever eating again — it was almost two! — the gym doors swung open and the cafeteria staff barreled in with metal carts.

"Sandwiches!" they bellowed, tossing the wax-paper-wrapped bundles up into the stands. It was madness.

Eventually Emily found a turkey and Swiss sandwich. Lewis managed to grab two — a roast beef and cheddar cheese and a boloney with American — which Emily didn't think was fair. But no sixth-grader ended up wailing about how he hadn't gotten a sandwich, so she figured it wasn't a big deal.

At three, when the final bell would normally ring, Dr. Franks stood up and shouted, "The eighth grade wins! See you tomorrow, children!"

* * *

"I don't know why she's not here yet," Emily said.

She and Lewis sat out front on the curb. All the buses had left, and Emily's mom still hadn't pulled up to drive her home. She offered Lewis a ride with them, but now, as the minutes ticked by, she wasn't sure her mom would ever show up.

"So I guess your phone isn't working?" Lewis asked.

Emily had been poking at it for the last thirty minutes, trying to get the number pad to come up so she could call her mom. But instead it only opened the web browser. It kept opening pages she'd never heard of, with long strings of random letters and numbers and even a bunch of characters she didn't recognize.

"Something's wrong with it," she said, smacking its side against the palm of her hand. "Stupid phone. This morning I couldn't get the alarm to stop, and now this. Piece of junk."

Lewis leaned back on his hands and looked up at the sky. "Everything's going crazy today," he said. "Not just your phone."

"Yeah," said Emily. She shoved her phone into her pocket. "Maybe everyone's uncle in IT is right after all."

Lewis laughed and stood up. "I'm tired of waiting."

Emily clucked her tongue. "You're just gonna leave me here?" she said.

"I'm going to the mall," Lewis said. "Come with me. There's a bus stop two blocks from here."

Emily stood up and wiped the street grit from her pants. "I know where the bus is," she said, "but I can't just take off to the mall without checking with —" She stopped herself, but it was too late.

"You have to check with Mommy and Daddy first?" Lewis said, obviously delighting in Emily's discomfort.

Emily snorted and crossed her arms. She could march home right now — it wasn't far, after all. But she hated the idea that Lewis would spend the afternoon sneering to himself because she acted like a scaredy-cat about everything.

"Fine," Emily said. She scooped up her bag and pulled it onto her shoulder. "Let's go to the mall, then."

Lewis laughed. "C'mon, don't be so grumpy about it," he said. "I bet your dad's there anyway, trotting around on his horse."

"What?" Emily said. "Why?"

He turned and headed for the school's front doors. "There's a grand opening today," Lewis said. "The mayor's going to be there. It's a big deal. I'm sure they'll have the mounted cops there, too."

"My dad didn't mention it to me," she said, hurrying alongside him to catch up. "Where are you going?"

Lewis shrugged. "You probably didn't ask," he said. "It's faster if we cut through to the back doors."

"I'm sure the doors are locked by now," Emily said, but before she'd even finished saying it, Lewis had swung open one of the front doors and headed inside. "Or not."

"It really is quicker," Lewis insisted. "Besides, those crazy Olympics were obviously meant to keep us students out of the classrooms all day. And I want to find out why."

The halls were dim and quiet. Their footsteps echoed off the metal lockers, smooth tiled walls, and high windows.

"It's weird when it's empty," Emily said.

"I guess," Lewis said. He tried the doors to a few classrooms. They were all locked. "This way."

"I know where the back door is," Emily said, but the truth was, she was spooked and had kind of forgotten where they were going.

They headed along the math wing. All the classroom doors in this corridor were locked, too. The math classrooms each had several expensive computers, smart boards, and tablets. Ms. Crenshaw would have been sure to lock every door, whether the faculty was trying to hide something or not.

But as Emily and Lewis walked by, flickering light escaped through the tall, narrow windows in each pale wooden door, and cast long, eerie shadows along the hallway.

"I don't like this," Emily said. She thought about grabbing Lewis's arm as she walked, like they were the stars of a horror movie, but she couldn't quite bring herself to.

He'd laugh, she thought.

It turned out he laughed anyway. "Don't be such a chicken," he said. "It's just the school, same as it always is, but with less people."

Emily let him walk on a bit and stopped to sneak a look into one of the empty, locked rooms.

The overhead lights were off and the blinds on the far side were pulled all the way down. Still the room was glowing with that eerie, flickering light of computer monitors.

Emily could see the displays of three computers that sat atop desks that were close to the door, facing the middle of the room. Words and numbers zipped by almost too fast to read. In fact, at first they seemed to Emily like random characters.

But then Emily spotted something that definitely wasn't random:

Terminal 147-A RBMS: Emily Lemon, 14. Reddish, wavy hair. Rosy cheeks. Red shoes. Yellow backpack. Lewis Cruz, 14. Dark brown hair. Large brown eyes. Headphones. Baggy black jeans. Green backpack. 01000001 01110000 01110000 01110010 01100101 01101000 01100101 01101110 01100100 00100000 01100001 01110100 00100000 01101000000010 . . .

Emily gasped and pulled away from the window. She pressed her back against the wall and held her breath.

"Lewis!" she hissed down the dark hallway. "Lewis!"

"What?" he said, not even bothering to stop. Not even bothering to turn around.

Emily took a last careful peek through the window to the classroom. Then she darted down the hall and caught up with Lewis.

This time, she did grab his arm, and she held it tight.

"What's wrong with you?" he asked. "Are you afraid of the dark now?"

"The computer back there," she said. "It was displaying information about us. About me and you. Our names. What we look like —" Emily stopped because Lewis's eyes had gone wide, not out of fear or concern, but out of disbelief.

She let go of his arm. "Fine," she said. "Never mind."

Maybe I am imagining it, she thought.

Either way, it wasn't like the computers in room 147 of the math wing could get up and run after her, right? Up ahead, sunlight poured in through the windows at the rear of the building. The double back doors, heavy and black and marked "Exit Only" in menacing red letters, were closed.

Emily jogged ahead and slammed them

open. She stepped outside into the sunny afternoon and sighed with relief as if she'd spent a hundred years underground.

Lewis came out a few seconds later. "Weirdo," he said, striding past her.

But Emily didn't care. The grassy hill sloped up toward Gilbert Avenue. She could see the slightly bent Bus Stop sign at the nearby corner.

Smiling, she hurried after Lewis.

CHAPTER 7

The bus ride from the middle school to the mall — which was free that day, thanks to a broken fare box — was about twenty minutes long. Aside from Lewis, Emily, and the driver, the bus was empty. And every bus stop they passed on the route was empty, too. They didn't spot a single person waiting to get on.

"Last stop," the driver said, his voice flat, bored, and weary. "Everyone out."

The brakes and doors hissed, and Emily and Lewis stepped out through the back door.

But they didn't find the busy, noisy mall they had expected. The parking lot was almost as empty as the bus had been. Only a few cars — none parked close to the mall — dotted the huge lot.

"So much for the big grand opening they were planning," Emily said. She pulled open the door to the mall and flashed a teasing smile at Lewis as she waved him inside. "Since there's not even a pigeon in sight, I assume the mayor and my dad aren't here either."

"I was sure it was today," Lewis said as he walked through the door she held for him.

Inside was as much of a wasteland as the parking lot had been. Though the stores seemed open, with their gates up and their lights on, there were no shoppers anywhere. And everything was eerily quiet — there wasn't even music playing over the stores' sound systems.

"I don't like this," Emily said.

Lewis took her hand. "It's weird," he said. "But it's not like something terrible is gonna happen, right?"

As he spoke, dim footsteps rang through the mall corridor. A man appeared from around the corner, walking fast and looking around nervously.

When he saw Emily and Lewis, he called to them. "I wouldn't shop today, kids!"

"Why?" Lewis asked. Then to Emily, he whispered, "I mean, it's not like it's too crowded, right?" The two of them giggled.

The man just shook his head and pushed through the doors to the parking lot outside. Before he left earshot, they heard him call for the bus to wait.

"Maybe we should just go home," Emily said. They moved slowly through the mall. All the stores looked fine — open, well lit, well stocked.

She didn't see any salespeople, though.

"Okay," Lewis said. He grabbed her hand and gave it a little squeeze. "Just come up to the food court with me real quick. I'm starving."

"Starving?" she snapped. "You had two sandwiches at lunch. That was less than three hours ago."

"What can I tell you?" Lewis said as he led her toward the escalator. "I'm a growing boy."

Emily rolled her eyes, but she followed. The escalators didn't seem quite right. One went up for a few steps, then stopped with a jerk and started going down. The one beside it did the opposite.

"I'm not getting on these things," Emily said.

Lewis looked around for a moment. "Hey, the elevator's right there, and the door is already open. Come on."

"Lewis," Emily said seriously. "I don't think it's a good idea."

"It'll be fine," he said, and then he pulled her by the hand.

Emily went to the far side of the elevator, where there was a big window that looked out over the first floor of the mall as they started to rise.

The food court was way up on the fourth floor, and as they went higher, Emily's view of the indoor amusement park in the center of the mall got wider and wider. She spotted all her favorites: the loop-the-loop roller coaster, the log chute, the salt and pepper shaker.

Several of the rides were still running, but they were all empty.

They do that sometimes, Emily told herself as she looked down on the scene. *Run the rides with no riders. It keeps the place looking fun and exciting.*

"Sorry," she said, turning from the window to face Lewis. "Sorry I freaked out — back at school and here, I mean."

Lewis shrugged. "Don't worry about it." Then he laughed a little. "Weird day, right?"

She nodded. "So weird."

The elevator dinged for the third time: fourth floor. Emily stood beside Lewis in front of the doors and waited for them to open.

And waited.

And waited.

Lewis gave the doors a little kick. "Open, stupid doors."

The elevator jerked a little.

"Don't kick it," Emily said.

The panel of buttons beside the door lit up, and the lights began to flash. The alarm went off — a shrill, metallic scream, and Emily could swear she felt the elevator shake, just a little. "What is happening?" she screamed over the alarm.

"I don't know!" Lewis said. He pounded his fists on the panel. "Open the doors, you stupid metal box!"

But the stupid metal box wouldn't listen. Emily imagined Lewis had only made it angrier.

But that's ridiculous, she told herself. *Technology doesn't get mad.*

She almost smiled. It had been a weird day, yes, but they weren't living in some sci-fi dystopia, after all. She checked the panel and noticed that the red alarm button was pushed in.

"Look," she said, calmer now, trying to speak over the screaming alarm. "You must have hit the emergency button by accident."

Emily leaned in front of Lewis and pushed the red emergency button again. The alarm stopped at once.

"See? No big deal," she said, but the moment the words left her lips, the elevator jerked again. The lights went off.

And they began to fall.

CHAPTER 8

If Emily had been shy about grabbing Lewis's arm before, she felt none of that now as the glass and steel box dropped five stories toward the mall's basement floor.

Emily threw her arms around Lewis, they held each other tight, and both of them screamed louder than they'd ever screamed in their lives.

"We're going to die!" Emily shrieked.

"I'm sorry!" Lewis screamed. "It's my fault!"

Emily shook her head at him. "No it's not! Don't say that!"

The elevator slammed into the basement floor. The windows smashed to bits, but the steel cage held together. Emily and Lewis crumpled to the floor, and the shattering glass splashed over them like a crystal waterfall.

But they were alive.

"Are you okay?" Lewis said. He climbed to his feet, brushed the shattered glass from his clothes, and helped Emily stand up.

"I think so," she said. She brushed the glass from her hair. "Ow!"

"Let me see," Lewis said.

Her hand was bleeding, but she let him take it and look at the long, fine-looking cut.

"It's not bad," he said. He pulled a bandana from his pocket. "It's clean, I promise." He wrapped it around her hand.

"Thanks," she said. "I can't believe we're okay."

Lewis looked in her eyes and nodded. "Let's see if we can get these doors open now."

Against hope, Emily leaned forward and pushed the "door open" button. The elevator didn't scream or beep. The doors simply slid open.

She took Lewis's hand in hers, still wrapped in his bandana, and they stepped out of the elevator. Whatever calm had washed over Emily when she realized they were both largely unhurt was long gone now. Her heart pounded as she recovered from the fall. Her hands sweated. Her skin tingled.

"Where are we?" Lewis asked.

"The basement of Grable's," Emily said. That was the big department store that took up most of the first floor of the mall. "I think."

But it was so dark, it was hard to tell. The ceiling lights were either dim and flickering or otherwise completely burnt out. The only steady bright light came from the red exit signs that hung here and there on the ceiling, pointing toward the ways out.

"This should be housewares," Emily said. She led Lewis into the reddish darkness. "Linens and gifts and silverware."

"You're right," Lewis said. Emily could feel it in his hand as he began to gain confidence. "That means the stairway should be that way."

Lewis pointed to a deep, dark corner of the department store basement. There was a doorway there. From where they stood, it looked to Emily like the mouth of a cave, and totally dark inside.

But above it, an exit sign shined red and bright, so Lewis was probably right.

"Okay," Emily said. "I guess we shouldn't bother finding someone to tell about the fallen elevator, right?"

Lewis might have smiled. It was hard to tell in the dim light. Then he said, "I get the feeling no one's around."

"Let's just get out of here," Emily said. "If there's an exit, I wanna go that way."

Nothing sounded better to Emily just then than the bright, fresh air of the outdoors. She should have rushed through the linen department, past the towels, and past the customer service desk, with Lewis running beside her.

But they moved slowly, like thieves sneaking past a slumbering dragon.

"I'm scared," Emily finally admitted. "But I don't know what I'm scared of."

"Me too," Lewis said. "And me neither."

It was so quiet. Emily could hear Lewis's breath. She could hear her own pulse — still racing from the fall. She could hear the air conditioner vents in the ceiling puffing their cool air.

She ran her hand over a display of towels as they walked slowly past. It was comforting: it reminded her of home. When she was younger — much, much younger — she'd play hide-and-seek with her dad, and she always hid in the bathroom closet. She'd press her face against the clean towels and wait for Dad.

Emily wished her dad were here now.

The stairwell was lit only by the orange emergency lights, probably powered by a generator that kicked on when all the electrics and computers in the mall had started acting crazy. Still, they reached the main floor without any more problems.

"The exit is this way," Lewis said. "It should lead to the south parking ramp . . . I think."

Emily didn't see any red exit signs right away. She let Lewis lead her through the shadowy darkness. They held hands as they walked through the children's clothing section.

It wasn't long ago that this was where Emily bought her clothes — or where her mom had bought clothes for her. Emily would go along on those trips, but she didn't have very strong opinions about clothes then.

She did now. Funny that the clothes in the kids' section seemed cuter to her now than they did then. Emily ran her hand over the soft fabric of toddler jammies and the stiff denim of little-kid overalls.

She and Lewis followed the winding path through the department store as it led them into the menswear section. Up ahead, an exit sign glowed red.

"We're going the right way," Lewis said, letting out a breath of relief.

But the menswear section glowed red under the exit sign. The mannequins were all dressed in dark suits, their featureless faces shining.

Emily shivered. "I'm glad those things aren't electrical," she said.

"What?" Lewis said.

Emily kept her eyes on the mannequins. "Doesn't it seem like everything electronic," she said, "everything computerized, is acting crazy today?"

"I guess," Lewis said. His grip on her hand tightened, and they walked on through the grim dark.

The toy department was next. Emily used to beg her mom to let her just look around in here. Even two years ago, she would have gathered up the few bills and coins she stored in a jar in her room — the one labeled "SPEND" — before a trip to Grable's Department Store. If Mom had been in a good and patient mood, Emily would spend as long as she could pacing the aisles of the toy section, obsessing over the apparently endless choices of baubles and dolls and building sets and action figures and race cars and plastic ponies and little electric bugs.

She hadn't stepped inside this toy section in ages. *When did I stop begging?* she wondered.

Maybe Lewis was thinking the same thing, but he didn't let on. He kept his eyes on the path, while hers wandered over the aisles of toys, and happy memories flooded her mind like the laughing gas she'd had at the dentist's office a couple times.

Those electric bugs. That doll that cries and crawls. That life-size dog that wags and fetches and barks and snarls. Those miniature soldiers with little guns that fire tiny plastic darts.

They're all electronic, Emily realized. "Lewis, they're all electronic."

"What?" Lewis said, not taking his eyes off the exit sign ahead.

Emily would have answered if she'd thought of how to answer or if she'd had the time. But the aisles of toys sprang to life — whirring and buzzing and clattering of plastic insect legs on metal shelves.

"Run!" she shouted, shoving Lewis along. But they weren't quick enough.

In seconds, boxes tore open. Plastic shells cracked. Dolls and soldiers and animatronic bears, dogs, unicorns, and dragons leapt down from their shelves and gave chase.

Tiny plastic missiles struck Emily in the face. She covered her eyes and shrieked.

"Don't stop," Lewis said, grabbing her hand again.

But the path in front of them was blocked now by a row of huge toy tanks and trucks. They all hummed and quivered, launching missile after missile. They swung cranes and front loaders as Emily and Lewis came closer.

Toys leapt down from the shelves that flanked the path out of the toy department. Soldiers and knights on horseback and near-life-size heroes and villains dove onto Emily's head and shoulders. They pounded their little plastic fists into her face.

"Get them off me!" she shouted, pulling at them, tugging them away. She grabbed one green-clad soldier and heaved him against the wall, where he smashed to pieces, his arm flying one way, his gun another, his head yet another.

But his little plastic body — with no head, with one arm — climbed to its feet and ran at her again. It pounded its fists into her shins and she stumbled.

The toys scratched. They bit. They grabbed hold of Emily's clothes. She pulled them off, though her clothes tore and her skin screamed in pain. She knew she would bruise. She knew she'd bleed. She didn't care.

More soldiers tangled in her hair and pulled at her clothes. The animatronic dog held her by the hem of her jeans and growled.

"Help me!" she called to Lewis.

Lewis had his own problems. He had been taken down already. He was on his stomach on the floor, and the toys climbed over him, pounded on him, and held him there, the trucks with their grippers, the insects with their pinchers, and the dinosaurs with their teeth.

Emily kicked and pulled the little toy monsters from her body. She threw toy after toy at the wall. They smashed to bits. Some got up again. Some didn't.

When they did, she kicked at them again and again. She pulled the dog from her jeans and swung him over her head. She let go, sending him flying back into the menswear section. She knew he wouldn't stay down long.

"Lewis," she said, "take my hand. Come on. You have to get up. You have to fight back."

She kicked at the living toys, freeing his arm and his legs. He took her hand and got to his feet. He grabbed the biggest one — a Tyrannosaurus rex toy with mad, glowing eyes and teeth as big as his own and ten times as sharp and deadly — and smashed it with his fist. Then he flung it against the shelves, sending another dozen toys sprawling to the floor.

"Run!" he yelled.

Though the toys gathered to block their way, Emily and Lewis pushed on. They ran through the barrier, kicking and grabbing at the toys as they went.

She smashed through, Lewis beside her. Soon they limped, battered and tired, out of the toy department, leaving behind them a fortune of toys destroyed.

CHAPTER 9

They were nearly out.

Emily could see pale daylight up ahead through three sets of double doors. "The exit," she said. "I hope we can catch another bus."

Lewis didn't say it, but Emily could tell he was thinking it, because she was too: there might not even be any busses running anymore. The one they'd taken here had been almost out of gas and hardly working.

But Emily couldn't think about that now.

Before they could even get to the double doors that led out of the mall, they had to cross through one more department. They stopped in the huge arched doorway. Above them hung a sign that sent a shiver up and down Emily's back.

HARDWARE.

"There has to be another way," she said. She looked back over her shoulder into the darkness, desperate to spot another red exit sign. There was one, barely visible, clear across the store.

"The other way out just leads back into the mall," Lewis said. "Besides, I don't really want to go back through that toy department."

Emily agreed with that. But still. "We have to find another exit. One that isn't near huge electric machines that will mow us down like an overgrown lawn!"

"Come on, Emily," Lewis said. "We can do this. Just keep your eyes on the exit sign. And keep moving."

Emily took a deep breath and nodded, and the two of them stepped through the archway.

"See?" Lewis said, reaching his hand out to grab Emily's. "Nothing to it."

Emily could hear the smile in his voice, but she couldn't smile herself. "Just keep walking," she said, keeping her eyes on the pale daylight through the doors. "I'll feel better when we're outside."

They were halfway through the big hardware department. In front of them sat power tools and paint cans. Behind them, the gleaming steel bodies of riding mowers and snowblowers.

"This isn't so bad," Lewis said. His hand around hers relaxed a little. But then, somewhere behind them, something clicked. Lewis's hand tensed.

"What was that?" Emily said. She looked over her shoulder — darkness.

"Nothing," Lewis said. "It sounded like — but I'm sure it was nothing."

"Sounded like what?" Emily asked even though she knew exactly what it sounded like.

Lewis walked faster. "Just keep walking," he said. "We're almost there."

Again from behind them came a click. Another click.

Lewis walked even faster. He held Emily's hand tighter.

"What is that?" Emily said. She wanted to scream, but in the terrifying hush, she dared not speak above a whisper.

Lewis still didn't answer, but Emily didn't have to wonder for long. The next sound was no mere click. Engines cranked and turned over, and motors came to life and screamed.

"Run!" Lewis shouted.

Emily didn't even turn around. She could see it all in her mind: a dozen riding mowers, powered up and shining their headlights over their victims, ready to run them down.

She ran. She held tight to Lewis's hand, and they ran past the towers of paint cans and hanging displays of brushes and screwdrivers and hacksaws — she felt grateful that the hacksaws weren't electric.

Behind them, the mowers squealed little rubber tires on the smooth tile floor, their blades and motors screaming. The beady headlights shined over their shoulders, leading the way to the doors with shaking beams of light.

"Almost there!" Lewis shouted over the din of motors and spinning blades.

They were close, but Emily nearly gave up. She nearly stopped running and let those mowers take her down. Because she spotted something Lewis hadn't: the doors were close, but they were bound with heavy chains.

They wouldn't get out that way.

Lewis reached the doors and shook them violently with both hands, as if with his brute strength he might shatter that chain and throw the doors open for them.

"We're trapped!" Lewis said. He slammed both his fists against the door's glass in anger.

Emily pressed her face to the glass and looked out into the empty quiet of the parking ramp. The light she'd seen hadn't been daylight after all, but the orange glow of the emergency lights in the walkway between the store and the parking ramp.

Staring through the door, she could also see the reflection of headlights charging from behind her: an army of mowers with two human targets.

Emily remembered the computer monitor back at the middle school — her and Lewis's names had been right there on the screen. She was finally convinced, whether someone's uncle in IT knew the truth or not, that the computers, all the technology, were rebelling.

Beside her, Lewis leaned on the chained doors. "We're done for," he said, and he let himself slump to the floor.

Emily nearly believed it. She almost slumped down next to him. But then she thought of something, and she smiled. "No way," she said, and she reached down and pulled Lewis up. "Get ready to jump."

"What?" he asked, and he climbed to his feet the same clumsy way Emily's big brothers climbed out of bed on a lazy Saturday morning.

"Trust me," she said. "Stand here. Take my hand. And get ready to jump."

Lewis looked at her like she was crazy. They were trapped, she knew, in this little entryway of the department store. The only way out was chained. And she wanted to face off against a small army of riding mowers?

But it would work. It had to work. She grabbed his hand. She crouched, ready to jump, and she counted off.

"Three," she said as the mowers roared through the paint department, knocking towers of paint cans down, sending splattering waves of Cornflower Blue and Goldenrod over the tile floor.

"Two," she said as the aisle of hacksaws and screwdrivers crashed to the floor.

"One!" she shouted over the noise as the army of mowers smashed down the sales rack near the doors.

"Now!" she screamed as the mowers roared into the entryway, and she tugged

Lewis with her as she leapt out of the way and behind a huge square column.

They ducked down as the mowers smashed the doors wide open and debris and bits of glass crashed into the entryway.

"Lewis, let's go. Let's get out of here!" Emily yelled.

Lewis was so scared, his eyes looked like they were about to pop out, but he got to his feet. Together, they climbed through the ruined set of doors and across the dimly lit walkway.

"We're out!" Lewis said. "I can hardly believe it!"

Emily smiled and grabbed his hand as they ran. She took a deep breath — the air smelled of tires, exhaust, and motor oil. She loved it.

Behind them, the mowers struggled to ride over the crushed steel of the doorway. They couldn't get through. It was over.

"You're a genius, Emily," Lewis said, and he slowed down to a jog.

Emily let herself relax and slowed down too. Together, they jogged through the parking ramp.

"More cars here than I would have guessed," Lewis said.

Emily scanned the lot. There weren't many — maybe twenty throughout the ramp — but he was right. They hadn't seen a single soul in that mall, aside from the man who'd warned them to leave.

They should have listened.

"I don't like this," Emily said. She stopped jogging and pulled Lewis to a stop, too.

"What?" he asked. "Let's just get to the bus stop."

She shook her head. Lights came on around them — headlights.

Engines clicked on and roared.

"The cars . . ." Emily said slowly. Her heart pounded and her skin prickled. "Lewis . . . the cars."

Tires squealed and echoed through the concrete ramp.

"We won't be able to outrun these, Lewis," Emily said in a whisper. She wanted to cry. She wanted to sob. She wished they had stayed in the towel department, where she could at least curl up and sleep. "What do we do?"

Lewis shook his head and took her hand. "We run," he said.

She could hardly move, never mind run, but she had no choice. They ran.

Behind them, the screeching of the car tires and the hum of the engines got louder as the cars raced through the winding ramp roadway.

"The stairs!" Lewis shouted over the noise. "They can't chase us there!"

And they couldn't. Emily had to let go of Lewis's hand as they shuffled down the steps as quickly as they could.

Lewis skipped every other step, but Emily couldn't. It was a bad dream she'd had as long as she could remember. She would always try to skip a step — everybody else could skip. But then she'd miss one, and her foot would slip, and she would flip over backward and fall the rest of the way down the stairs. She'd always wake up then, just before her head crashed onto the cement ground.

"All the way down," Lewis said as they stepped off the stairs on the next level. The cars roared to life there, too, as the cars from above came speeding and squealing down the ramp.

So they kept running, down another set of steep cement steps. Lewis was far ahead now, and Emily had to keep one hand on the railing as she went. Her head spun. Her hands sweated and slipped from the rail. Her feet didn't obey, and with every step she nearly tumbled to the bottom.

When she reached the ground floor, Lewis grabbed her shoulders and looked her in the face. "You're okay," he said. "But we have to keep running."

The wide-open bottom floor of the parking ramp lay before them. Only three cars waited here, and when Lewis and Emily, hand-in-hand, stepped out of the orange-lit stairwell, they roared to life.

The cars started coming at them from all different directions, and soon they were joined by the vehicles from the floors above that had made their way down to the ground floor. Emily looked back at the stairwell, thinking she could sprint there for safety, but one of the cars was now blocking the way.

"Run, Emily! We have to run!" Lewis shouted, tugging her by the arm.

But it was no use. She couldn't keep up. "I can't," she said with the little breath she could gather. She let Lewis's hand slip from hers and turned to face the oncoming cars.

Their headlights bounded and danced in the low light of the parking ramp.

Their engines screamed as they picked up more and more speed. This would be the end. At least she wouldn't have to run anymore.

CHAPTER 10

Lewis grabbed Emily by the wrist. "I'm not going to just let you stand there and get run over!" he shouted.

Emily pulled her arm back. "It's hopeless!" she yelled over the roar of engines. "There's nowhere to run!"

Lewis looked desperately around. "The mall!" he said. "We can go back inside the mall!"

Emily almost laughed. The cars were only a hundred yards away now — maybe less. "Why?" she said. "So the floor waxers can get us? They're everywhere, Lewis. Or did you plan to run all the way to the North Woods?"

The vehicles were so loud now, their motors thundering and echoing, filling her ears with the charging thunder of death.

But there was something else. Hidden by the rumbling of motors and the screeching of rubber on cement, there was a familiar and even comforting sound.

It echoed from behind her. Clip-clop, clip-clop, clip-clop.

Emily spun, letting the cars bear down on her with her back to them, and she nearly sobbed at what she saw.

"Dad," she said, barely a whisper. Then she shouted and ran toward him as he galloped toward her. "Dad!"

Lewis ran behind her — she heard the slap of his sneakers on the cement. But she didn't look back. She didn't stop. She ran faster than she'd ever run before.

"Give me your hand!" Dad shouted, reaching down from his saddle.

Emily reached out to him and let him pull her up. She slipped into the saddle behind him and wrapped her arms around his waist.

"You too!" Dad shouted, holding his hand out to Lewis. He pulled Lewis up, and before the boy had even gotten seated, he urged the horse on with a kick and a raspy, "Heeya!"

They galloped away. Dad urged his horse on. She jumped a low wall to leave the parking ramp. Emily twisted to watch as the cars smashed into the cement and steel, creating a pile-up of twenty cars or more. She even laughed.

Lewis shouted past her ear, "Where are we going, Mr. Lemon?"

"Far away from the city," he shouted back without turning around. "Mom's already there, Emily. And the boys. Your mom, too, Lewis."

Emily hugged tight around her dad.

They galloped on, away from the mall, the highways, the neighborhoods, the train line, the houses, and the traffic lights. They rode on until the sun was down and the moon was high and the only sound they heard was the soft rhythm of the horse's hooves and the singing of crickets.

CHAPTER 11

The old woman coughed into her fist. "That's how it all started," she said. "That girl, that boy, their families, and a few others. We gathered here, and we made our way."

"That was you?" said the teen girl sitting across the campfire from the old woman. "You're Emily?"

She laughed. "I haven't gone by that name in years," she said. "First it was Emily, then Emmy, then Milly. Now I'm usually Mum or Grandmum. And I know there are a few other less flattering names as well."

Her eyes twinkled in the flickering light of the campfire. "I'm off to bed," she said. "You kids better get to bed soon, too. You'll have to work in the morning, yes?"

She slowly got to her feet with the help of her knotty walking stick, worn smooth under years of use. Bent and tired, she smiled down at them. "We're doing all right, aren't we?" she asked.

"Yes, ma'am," said the teen boy who sat beside his girlfriend. He put his arm around her shoulders. "Good night, Mum."

She smiled again, though her eyes looked wet, and slowly she tottered away along the path to the little house in their little village, her home for the last eighty years.

When she'd gone, and when the silence of the night had fallen over the campfire so they could hear every chirp in the woods and every pop and crack in the fire, the girl turned to her boyfriend.

"Do you believe her?" she asked. "Do you believe that story?"

The boy shrugged one shoulder. "She's a crazy old lady," he said. "You can't believe everything she says."

"Right," said another boy. He laughed. "She once told me about this thing that used to hang in her house. A painting sort of, but the pictures moved and were never the same."

"See?" said the boyfriend. "Crazy old lady."

"I don't know," the girl said. "She didn't seem crazy to me."

"I like her," said another girl.

"So you don't believe the story?" the girlfriend asked.

Her boyfriend sat up straight with a huff. "Do I believe her? Do I believe that the machines used to work for us, instead of us working for them?" he asked.

"Right," said his girlfriend.

He thought for a second. "No," he said firmly. "No way."

"Why not?" she asked, looking down the empty path that led to the old lady's house.

"Why would people build things like that?" he said. "I mean, even if we could build them, why would we?"

"He's right," said another girl. "Anyone could have guessed this would happen if we made things more powerful and more intelligent than we are."

The girl took her boyfriend's hand. She stared into the fire. "I guess you're right," she said.

She lifted her head and looked out over the woods toward the shining light of the city, two days' walk away, where the electronic masters lived. She shivered, because the city kept spreading, and soon they would have to move.

GLOSSARY

animatronic (AN-uh-muh-TRAW-nik) — animated by something electronic

assembly (uh-SEM-blee) — a meeting with a lot of people

computerized (kuhm-PYOO-tuh-rized) — controlled by means of a computer

dystopia (diss-TOH-pee-yuh) — an imaginary world where people are unhappy and often fear for their lives

generator (JEN-uh-RAY-tur) — a machine that produces electricity by turning a magnet around inside a coil of wire

hardware (HAHRD-wair) — tools and equipment that are most often used in the house or yard

mannequins (MAN-i-kin) — life-sized models of humans, often used in stores to display clothing

mastermind (MAS-tur-minde) — a person who plans and controls an activity, often a harmful one

metallic (meh-TAL-ik) — relating to or resembling metal

misbehaving (MIS-bi-HAYV-ing) — acting poorly or inappropriately

overlords (OH-vur-lords) — rulers who have great power over many people

rebelling (ri-BELL-ing) — opposing against a ruler

wasteland (WAYST-land) — an area that is barren or empty

DISCUSSION QUESTIONS

1. Why do you think the teachers weren't honest with the students about what was going on at Roaring Brook Middle School? Discuss the possibilities.

2. By the end of the story, Emily Lemon is terrified of all technology. Have you ever been afraid of technology? What was it that scared you and why?

3. Talk about how your understanding and appreciation of Grandmum and the villagers changed from the beginning of the book to the end. How would the story have been different if Grandmum and the villagers were not included?

WRITING PROMPTS

1. When Emily and Lewis enter the mall, a man warns them that they should probably leave, but they don't listen. How do you think the story would've turned out if Emily and Lewis had left right away? With that in mind, write another possible ending to the story.

2. Technology can be complicated and can often cause unintended problems (like a power outage, for example). Write about a time when some piece of technology (a phone, a light, a computer, a TV, etc.) did not work the way you expected it to. What did it do? How did you fix it?

3. What is your favorite piece of technology? Write one paragraph about what you love about it, and write another paragraph about how your life would be different without it.

ABOUT THE AUTHOR

Eric Stevens lives in St. Paul, Minnesota. He is studying to become a middle-school English teacher. Some of his favorite things include pizza, playing video games, watching cooking shows on TV, riding his bike, and trying new restaurants. Some of his least favorite things include olives and shoveling snow.

ABOUT THE ILLUSTRATOR

Nelson Evergreen lives on the south coast of the United Kingdom with his partner and their imaginary cat. Evergreen is a comic artist, illustrator, and general all-around doodler of whatever nonsense pops into his head. He contributes regularly to the British underground comics scene, and he is currently writing and illustrating a number of graphic novel and picture book hybrids for older children.

MAD SCIENCE

Humankind's ingenuity and creativity is one of its defining features. We're constantly trying to improve the world around us. But what happens when we push the limits of technology and science? Will we be left trying to outrun murderous lawn mowers? Maybe not, but the fear of technology and our own inventiveness has been a constant source of anxiety throughout much of history.

The Industrial Revolution was a period ripe for emerging fears of technology. Between the mid-1700s and the early 1800s, England experienced a sudden boom in industry. Breakthroughs of all kinds meant that machines could make things faster and cheaper. But the new, efficient machines were replacing people, and many skilled workers were left without a job. A group known as the Luddites strongly opposed the new technology, and they rioted and sabotaged machines. Although there aren't really riots against machines nowadays, people still fear that new technology will take their jobs, and maybe one day even completely replace human labor. The term "Luddite" is actually used now more generally to refer to someone who opposes technological advancement.

During the Industrial Revolution, one of the first science fiction novels was published, and it warned against science and technology overstepping its boundaries. In her famous novel, *Frankenstein; or, The Modern Prometheus,* Mary Shelley tells the story of a scientist who tries to play God by giving life. As we know, it does not end well for Victor Frankenstein, and his misuse of science creates a murderous monster.

In more recent times, we've continued to fear that we will go too far in our scientific pursuits. World War II and the creation and dropping of the atomic bomb showed us how dangerous and deadly our inventions could be. And now with an abundance of smart technology, plenty of movies and books, it is easy to imagine a world where we make our devices too smart.

Will our creations become so intelligent that they find humans to be unnecessary and in the way, like HAL 9000 did in *2001: A Space Odyssey*? Or will we become too dependent on our gadgets, like in *WALL-E*? Or perhaps technology won't lead to a dystopia at all, but will continue to be a useful, everyday tool. Only time will tell.

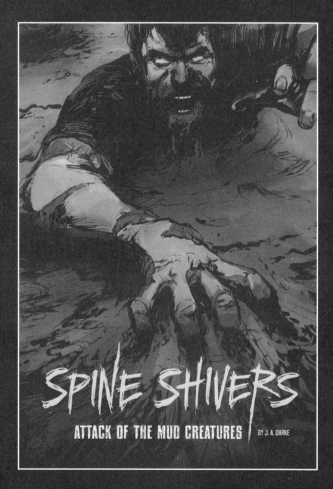

SPINE SHIVERS

ATTACK OF THE MUD CREATURES

BY J. A. DARKE

ATTACK OF THE MUD CREATURES

"Grey!" Trevor shouted from the bottom of the broken stairs. "Oh man, I was hoping you'd find me."

As Grey's eyes grew accustomed to the darkness of the basement, he saw that his friend's legs were buried up to the shin in mud and muck, like the earth had clawed its way up and held fast to him.

"But — but you're . . ." Grey couldn't wrap his mind around what he saw. He'd just spoken with Trevor, trapped in the basement of a house an entire block away. He'd run here to call for help. Finding Trevor in *this* house, in *this* basement? It just didn't make sense.

"You have to help me," Trevor said, reaching out his arm. "Get me out of here."

"What's going on?" Grey asked. "How are you *here*?"

"I was talking to Mira, and then . . . I saw something. Here at the house. So I came up to check it out and . . . it trapped me."

"What trapped you?"

"The house. The mud. There's something in the *mud*," Trevor said. "It's taking us over, one by one — sucking us down into the ground and creating clones out of the earth. I saw it . . . it *made* a version of me."

That's not possible, Grey told himself.

Grey didn't believe in any of that supernatural garbage. Aliens? Lame.

Bigfoot? A guy in a suit. Ghosts? People seeing what they wanted to see. So his brain struggled to understand how there were two Trevors. He didn't believe what his friend was telling him.

Not until the house began to move on its own.

The stucco wall beside Grey shuddered and expanded. It pressed in toward him, like a bulging, bubbling mass. Grey stumbled backward, tripped over his feet, and fell to the floor. He brought one arm up to protect his eyes in case the bubble popped.

It didn't. The bulging mass on the wall changed shape, and he could see that it was clay and mud.

The house is made of mud.

Grey looked down at his hands, which were pressed against the kitchen's tile floor. He curled his fingers, scratching at the dirty tiles as dirt caked under his nails.

We have to get out of here.

He staggered to his feet. Outside, a clap of thunder shook the house. The rain was coming down harder now. Grey heard it against the roof and the walls. He pictured the mud house crumbling to wet chunks of earth, burying Trevor and him underneath it.

"There is no escape," a woman's voice said. Grey looked up. The mass on the wall had formed into the shape of a human face, and it was staring back at him.

He was looking right at Mary.

It didn't look entirely like the real Mary, the one Grey had first met, the one who cried about losing her photo albums. The face in the wall was not completely formed. It was unlined, too smooth to be human. And the eyes looked tired, hollow.

All of them, he thought, remembering Mary and the man at the community center and every other soul he'd seen looking tired and empty and lost. *They've all been replaced by whatever is lurking in the ground.*

Mary's face smoothed and disappeared, the mud molding itself into another face. This time, Grey was looking at Summer. It changed again, and he saw Andy. It changed once more, and he was looking at himself.

"Grey? Are you still there?!" Trevor called.

Hearing his friend's voice snapped Grey back from the shock that was threatening to envelope him. "Yeah," he said. "I'm here." He staggered forward, his eyes never leaving the wall and its horrifying mirror image of himself. He reached the open doorway and crouched down.

"Can you reach up?" he asked, stretching his arm toward Trevor as far as he possibly could. Trevor leaned forward, trying unsuccessfully to pull himself out of the mud. Their hands were mere inches apart.

"I can't . . . reach you," Grey said. "I can't do it."

"You can," Trevor said. "I know you can."

Grey lay flat on his stomach, momentarily forgetting that the floor on which he now lay was part of whatever living, moving creature trapped Trevor. He reached his arm out.

"We're not . . . gonna make it out of here," Grey said.

Trevor's hand snaked up and clamped down on Grey's wrist. "Yes, we are," Trevor said. "Everything is just fine."

Everything is just fine.

The words turned Grey's blood cold. He'd heard them before. From the man at the community center. From Mary.

No. Not Trevor, too.

Grey pulled his arm back toward him. Caught by surprise, Trevor lost his grip. "Dude, what are you doing?" he asked.

Grey shook his head. "You're not Trevor, are you?"

"Of course I am. Come on. I'm your best friend, Greyson."

"You're trying to trick me," said Grey. "This is all one big game, isn't it?"

He stood, stumbled back a step.

Down in the basement, Trevor smiled. It was a wicked grin. The lines on his face disappeared, and the mud at his feet receded back into the ground. "Join us, Greyson," it said, its voice cold and calculating and not at all Trevor's anymore.

SPINE SHIVERS